A science

The Magic School Bus®
CHAPTER BOOK
AMAZING MAGNETISM

SCHOLASTIC INC.
New York   Toronto   London   Auckland   Sydney
Mexico City   New Delhi   Hong Kong   Buenos Aires

Written by Rebecca Carmi.

Illustrations by John Speirs.

Based on *The Magic School Bus* books
written by Joanna Cole and illustrated by Bruce Degen.

The author and editor would like to thank Professor Eric Brewe of Arizona State
University for his advice in preparing this manuscript.

ISBN 0-439-31432-1

60 59 58 57 56 55 54 53 52 51 50   16/0

Designed by Peter Koblish

Printed in the U.S.A.   40

INTRODUCTION

My name is Carlos. I am one of the kids in Ms. Frizzle's class.

Maybe you have heard of Ms. Frizzle. (Sometimes we just call her the Friz.) She is a terrific teacher — but strange. One of her favorite subjects is science, and she knows everything about it.

She takes us on lots of field trips in the Magic School Bus. Believe me, it's not called *magic* for nothing! We never know what's going to happen when we get on that bus.

Ms. Frizzle likes to surprise us, but we

can usually tell when she is planning a special lesson — we just look at what she's wearing.

One day she came into class wearing a dress covered with what looked like a bunch of horseshoes. But when I looked closer, I realized they were horseshoe magnets. That was how I knew we were about to study magnetism. Little did we know how many different things magnets do. We discovered they're everywhere. But let me start from the beginning. . . .

CHAPTER 1

I was running through the hallway to get to Ms. Frizzle's classroom. We were starting a new study unit and I couldn't wait to find out what it was. But as I rounded the corner, I ran straight into something. I hit it with such a thud that I fell backward. Ouch! As I landed, I felt a button pop off my shirt and saw it roll away. I went to grab the button, but then I stopped. Sitting on the floor, facing me was Andrew Cochran, my least favorite person. Now I knew what, actually *who*, I ran into. I couldn't believe my bad luck.

Andrew was Mr. O'Neatly's star pupil.

Mr. O'Neatly was the other third-grade teacher. He and Ms. Frizzle sometimes shared study units together. Last month we had a spelling bee. I didn't like to think too much about it. Because of me, our class had lost. And because of Andrew, Mr. O'Neatly's class had won. He'd correctly spelled the word that I'd missed — *attraction*.

"Watch where you're going," Andrew said as he started picking up his books. The one on top had a big picture of a horseshoe on it and the title was *All about Magnets*.

"Sorry," I mumbled as I scrambled to my feet. I slung my backpack over my shoulder and started toward class. I didn't even stop to look for the missing button. Andrew liked to remind me of his spelling-bee victory almost every day, and I wanted to get away before he had a chance to tell me again.

I wasn't fast enough. "We're going to beat you again!" he called as I ran off.

I wondered what he meant. I sure hoped we weren't having another spelling bee!

When I got into class I saw that the geography signs from our last unit were still up. Over Ms. Frizzle's desk was a big sign that read WEST. Over the windows was a sign that read NORTH and behind me a sign that read EAST. Over the door the sign read SOUTH. But I noticed that Ms. Frizzle wasn't wearing her map dress anymore. Her new dress was covered with the same horseshoe shapes as Andrew's book!

"Good morning, class," she sang out. "Today we are going to start a most *attractive* unit!" Oh, no, that reminded me of the word *attraction* again.

Ms. Frizzle held up a large horseshoe magnet. It wasn't hard to guess that our new unit was going to be about magnetism.

Then we noticed that on everyone's desk was a little box with stuff in it — a bumpy rock, a rubber band, a plastic checker piece, some paper clips, a piece of paper, a nail, a penny, and a black rectangular bar magnet.

"This will be easy, Carlos," Wanda whispered. "All we'll have to do is pick up things with magnets."

"Yeah," I whispered back. "Nothing to it."

We should have known better. When was anything straightforward in Ms. Frizzle's class?

I looked around the room. Some of the other kids had chains of paper clips hanging from their magnets. Others were trying to pick up stuff like paper and rubber bands, but it wasn't working, of course. Anyone knows magnets only pick up metal things.

"Class," said Ms. Frizzle with a big smile, "Mr. O'Neatly and I thought the best way to learn about magnets would be to have a little contest."

Everyone groaned. Mr. O'Neatly's class always beat us. Our class lost the spelling bee, the kickball tournament, the pumpkin-pie baking contest, and the summer readathon. No wonder Andrew was smug.

"Don't worry, kids," said the Friz. "If there's one thing our class can do well, it's science. And this is a science scavenger hunt. It's our turn to show our science stuff!"

"Yeah, we'll leave them behind this time," I said, thinking of beating Andrew.

"Take out the piece of paper in your box," Ms. Frizzle said, "and we can begin the science scavenger hunt!"

On the paper was a list of riddles. They must be the scavenger hunt clues, I thought.

"Whichever class fills out the list first wins a pizza party. The winner is the class that brings the completed list to the science lab first," said the Friz. She didn't have to say another word. We all had our lists out and were busily reading. I read the first riddle.

Scavenger Hunt Question #1
A magnet picks me up.
A magnet holds me high.

I'm not paper, wood, or rubber.
I'm not plastic — what am I?

"What's that supposed to mean?" Phoebe asked.

"It's asking what's attracted to magnets," said Tim. "That's easy. It's metal."

"Oh, yeah?" said Ralphie. "What about the penny? It's metal. And look. The magnet can't pick it up at all." He held his penny next to the magnet, let go, and the penny clinked to the floor.

"Hmmm," I said, feeling stumped. I worried that Andrew had found the answer to the riddle already.

Then we noticed Dorothy Ann flipping through the pages of a book. It was the same as Andrew's — *All about Magnets*. D.A. always seemed to have a book, and she usually knew a lot about our new science units before everyone else.

"Here's the answer," she said, reading from the book. "Magnets attract only a certain kind of metal."

From *All about Magnets*
Magnet Metals

Magnets are only attracted to metals. Metals that contain iron and steel attract magnets well. Metals like brass, copper, zinc, and aluminum are not attracted to magnets.

"So magnets don't attract copper," Tim said. "That's why the penny didn't stick."

"Yes," said D.A., still reading from the book. "Pennies are made of copper-coated zinc."

"I'll write down the answers as we find them," I said. I wanted to make sure the answers were written down correctly. This was one race we weren't going to lose to Mr. O'Neatly's class if I had anything to do with it. I whisked out my pen and wrote: *Metals that contain iron and steel stick to magnets.* That was the answer to number one. Only nine more to go! I could already taste the pizza.

CHAPTER 2

Arnold was playing with the contents of his box. Just as I finished writing the answer, he said, "Hey! My paper clips are sticking to this bumpy old rock!"

I quickly took the paper clip on my desk and held it against the rock. It stuck! "What's going on, Ms. Frizzle?" I asked.

"Well, you know that iron and steel stick to magnets, so what does that tell you about the rock?" asked Ms. Frizzle.

"It's a magnet?" said Wanda. "It doesn't look like one."

"But it acts like one," said Keesha.

"That's right. And when we do scientific

experiments, we have to trust our observations," said the Friz.

"So these old rocks are magnets?" asked Tim. "What does your book say, D.A.?"

D.A. found a picture of one of our rocks in the book.

From *All about Magnets*

Magnetite is a natural magnet. People first found out about magnetism when they discovered the magnetic power of these rocks.

"And look at the second question of the scavenger hunt!" I said.

Scavenger Hunt Question #2
We look the same as rocks,
But we don't act the same.
We are natural magnets.
Can you guess our name?

As I finished reading, Phoebe said, "Magnetic rocks! The rocks on our tables."

"Yeah," said Tim. "So the answer to the riddle is magnetite!"

I carefully picked up the scavenger hunt list and wrote down: *Magnetite is a rock that is a natural magnet.*

History of Magnets
by Wanda

The first people to discover magnetic rocks were the Chinese. They called it "the loving stone" because the stones love metal the way parents love children. At first the Chinese used the stones to perform fortune-telling and magic tricks. Later they used the loving stones to invent the compass — hundreds of years before the Europeans.

I carefully folded the scavenger list and put it in my pocket. I had a good feeling about this. We already had two answers! We might even beat Mr. O'Neatly and Andrew this time.

CHAPTER 3

"It's time to get serious! Follow me to the science lab," said the Friz. "Mr. O'Neatly and I have set up some experiments to help us find the answers. Bring your magnetic kits with you." Then Ms. Frizzle picked up a fancy remote control box with a picture of the Magic School Bus on it, gave it a little pat, put it in a bag, and slung it over her shoulder.

We looked at one another. What was our teacher doing with a remote control? The Friz always had a plan.

We passed Mr. O'Neatly's class on the way to the lab. His classroom was right next door to ours. Now we pretended not to look, but

I know I wasn't the only one who took a peek. Mr. O'Neatly's students were still hanging paper clips from magnets. We were ahead! We went around two corners to the lab.

Ms. Frizzle told us to get a partner and go to a table. Arnold and I headed for a table set up with a large bar magnet and some needles.

Ms. Frizzle rummaged in her bag for something. "Now, where are those iron filings?

I thought I put them in here." She unloaded a few things from her bag, including the fancy remote control with a picture of the Magic School Bus on it. Then she shook her head and looked around the room.

"What do they look like?" I asked, looking around the lab.

"Iron filings are small pieces of iron, like tiny pins. They are perfect for experiments. Ahh. Here's a brand-new box of iron filings!" She picked up a box off the center table, opened it, and shook out a bunch of small metal pieces. Each of us took a small handful and put them on our tables.

"First of all, stroke the needle from your kits with the magnet and see what happens," said the Friz. I could see Wanda at the next table. She stroked the needle against the magnet and put it down on the table. As soon as she set it down, all the iron filings near the needle flew toward it and stuck.

"The needle turned into a magnet!" I said.

"Carlos, ours isn't working," said Arnold. The Friz came over and looked.

"You have to stroke in only one direction, Arnold," she said.

Ms. Frizzle stroked our needle against a large magnet. "You see, anything with iron in it can be magnetized." She picked up several iron filings with our needle and handed it to us. "Then it becomes a temporary magnet."

"Wow," I said. "That's so cool." I took the magnetized needle and used it to pin my shirt together where the button had popped off. "That's another way to use a magnet to stick things together," I whispered to Arnold.

My mind had started to wander, but Arnold poked me and said, "Wake up, Carlos. We have to know this stuff to win the contest."

He was right. I didn't want to miss the next question. Not when we were in the lead! I read the next question.

Scavenger Hunt Question #3
Not all magnets start on the ground.
Not all magnets have to be found.

When you do this very easy chore,
You can use one magnet to make many more.

"What's the chore, kids?" asked Ms. Frizzle.

"It's what we did to make the needles into magnets," said Keesha.

"Right!" I said. "And I know what to write!"

I took out the scavenger list and wrote very carefully. *If you stroke a needle with a magnet in one direction, the needle will become a magnet.*

But that wasn't enough for D.A. She had to know more.

"What's happening inside the needle?" she asked. "Why does it attract the iron filings?"

That got Ms. Frizzle started. Did I say this magnet stuff was going to be easy? Well, I was wrong.

"Let's find out!" beamed the Friz. "As I always say, to understand an iron filing, you have to become an iron filing."

Arnold moaned.

"Can't D.A. just read to us from her book some more?" he asked in a small voice. I noticed that Arnold's voice was getting smaller and smaller as he spoke.

And I felt myself shrinking. . . .

"Whoa!" I said. I looked down at myself and at the others. We were all iron filings! We were supersmall — even the Friz was tiny. We

still had heads and arms and legs, but our bodies were made of metal.

"Now, Liz will walk around with a magnet and you can all see what it feels like to be attractive."

At that moment, Liz, who was still her normal size, dropped the large magnet she was carrying and scampered under the center table. "What's wrong, Liz?" said Ms. Frizzle, but then she stopped. We all heard it at the same time. Footsteps. And voices. It was Mr. O'Neatly and his class.

As they came through the door I groaned. Andrew was right behind Mr. O'Neatly. They all looked enormous from the point of view of an iron filing.

"Don't worry, class," said the Friz. She was holding the fancy remote control. "I'm calling the Magic School Bus here to rescue us." Then she pushed a button with a picture of the bus on it. "It'll be here in a jiffy."

We could hear Mr. O'Neatly's voice booming above us.

"Yes, Andrew, part of good science is preparing your materials in advance," Mr. O'Neatly was saying.

He stopped walking. "Look at the state of this place! What happened?" he said indignantly. All of our magnetic kits were still spread over the lab tables. "I can't bear a messy lab. It was perfectly clean this morning. And I left a box of brand-new iron filings right here on the table. . . ." Mr. O'Neatly stopped and looked at the empty table where Ms. Friz had unloaded her bag. Oops, I could pretty much guess what happened: Ms. Frizzle had taken Mr. O'Neatly's box of filings!

"Now where could they have gone?" Mr. O'Neatly stomped around the table, peering underneath it. His footsteps shook the floor and made us vibrate. We huddled together on the floor.

"Mr. O'Neatly, there are some iron filings on the floor," said Andrew eagerly, pointing down at us. Andrew leaned toward us. At that moment I saw the miniature Magic

School Bus pop out of a vent in the wall behind Andrew. It was moving fast.

"Hurry up, hurry up!" I said to myself. The bus was speeding toward us, but it had to cross the whole lab.

"Very well," said Mr. O'Neatly. "Someone must have spilled them." The bus was almost in front of us when Mr. O'Neatly kneeled down. The Magic School Bus ran up against Mr. O'Neatly's shoe just as he swept us all into his hand.

"Whoa," I yelled as his giant hand closed around us.

"Hey, look at this," said Andrew, pointing to the Magic School Bus.

Mr. O'Neatly sighed. "Leaving toys on the floor is a terrible habit. I dislike having to clean up after a certain other class all the time." He leaned back down and, with his other hand, scooped up the Magic School Bus.

"All of you can take a seat and stroke your needles with a magnet, as I explained." The class of giants moved to our magnetic kits. "Be sure to stroke in one direction," he called out. With a sinking heart I realized they were catching up to us, while we were stuck in Mr. O'Neatly's hand.

But then things got worse. "You see, class," he said. "Anything with iron or steel in it can be magnetized, like this toy. Notice that I am stroking it with this magnet. Now it's a magnet, too, and it will stick to the refrigerator."

I couldn't believe Mr. O'Neatly turned our escape vehicle into a refrigerator magnet. Being around Mr. O'Neatly's class was always bad luck. And I could tell Andrew was working hard to win the scavenger hunt.

"But Mr. O'Neatly," said Andrew. "Why does it become a magnet?"

"That's just what I wanted to know," whispered Dorothy Ann.

"Why don't you consult the book, Andrew?" said Mr. O'Neatly. He looked pleased that Andrew had asked such an intelligent question.

Andrew flipped through *All about Magnets* and found the right page.

From _All about Magnets_
What's Inside a Magnet?

A piece of iron or steel contains atoms. Each atom has electrons dancing around the center. The way the electrons dance is called the atom's domain.

In magnets, the domains all point in the same direction. In things that aren't magnets, the domains point in different directions.

This is not a magnet.
The domains are not lined up.

This is a magnet.
The domains are lined up.

"So, class," Mr. O'Neatly said, "when the needle is stroked with a magnet, the magnet's force makes its domains line up. Then, the needle is a magnet, too."

I couldn't follow Mr. O'Neatly at all. Our chances for the scavenger hunt weren't looking good.

CHAPTER 4

From the inside of Mr. O'Neatly's hand, we heard his muffled voice.

"Okay, class," Mr. O'Neatly said as he dumped us on a table. "Now that you've all magnetized your needles, Andrew is going to help me demonstrate what the shape of a magnetic field looks like. Gather round."

Mr. O'Neatly's class gathered in a circle around us. They looked awfully big and scary, staring down at us.

"Class, watch carefully as Andrew spreads the iron filings out on a piece of paper. By noticing where the filings go, you will see where the magnet creates a magnetic field," said Mr. O'Neatly. He poured us into Andrew's outstretched hands.

"Be careful not to touch any of the iron filings to the magnet," said Mr. O'Neatly. "Those filings are so small, you might never get them off." Now I was really worried — we were at Andrew's mercy!

Magnetic Field Trip
by Mr. O'Neatly

The field of force around a magnet is called a magnetic field. An object within this area will be pulled toward the magnet. The field is strongest at the ends of a magnet and weakest in the middle. You can see the shape of a magnetic field by placing iron filings on a piece of paper over a magnet. The iron filings will be drawn to the magnet in the shape of the magnetic field.

Andrew tossed us onto a piece of paper and held a bar magnet underneath us.

"Whoa!" we all yelled as we suddenly got pushed and pulled around. I tried to stay where I was because I wanted to keep Mr. O'Neatly's class from getting the answer, but the pull was irresistible! It felt like something was pulling me by my head and my feet at the same time. And it wasn't just that I was moving — my insides seemed to be turning around. It was worse than the wildest roller coaster I'd ever been on!

"Ohh," groaned Arnold. "Why is my stomach swirling around?"

"Your domains are lining up with the magnetic field," said Ms. Frizzle from the other side of the magnet.

"My what?" asked Arnold.

"Your domains: the parts of your iron-filing body that make you magnetic. In most things, the domains face in all different directions. But the domains in iron and steel are different. When iron and steel are exposed to a magnet, the magnet's pull forces the domains

to all line up the same way," said the Friz in her science-class voice. "That's how magnets attract metals."

"Great," said Arnold. "But it still makes me nauseous. I feel like my insides are twisting."

"That's exactly what's happening!" said the Friz with great excitement. Everyone was complaining about how it felt when the domains were lining up. Ralphie said it was worse than a broken leg. Keesha said it just tickled.

Then I overheard what Mr. O'Neatly was saying to his class. It was obvious that they were quickly catching up, and that made me feel sick all over again. My body had already turned into iron, then it was practically turned inside out as my domains were lined up. What else would we have to do to win the scavenger hunt? I was exhausted, but D.A. still had plenty of questions.

"But how do we know the electrons are lined up?" asked D.A.

"Well, scientists can't see electrons in even the most powerful microscope," said the

Friz. "But if I push this button," she said as she moved her thumb, "*we* can see electrons."

We looked down at our bodies. Rows of blue lights were blinking on and off. "What's that?" I asked.

"I lit up all the electrons in the room," said the Friz. I looked around. There were blinking blue lights everywhere, but the lights were only in straight rows inside of us and inside the magnet. "Your electrons are lined up and pulling together. If you look around, you'll see that in all the nonmagnetic materials in the room, the electrons are just scattered."

"Cool! Now we can answer number four!" said Ralphie, who was holding his scavenger list out with his free hand.

Scavenger Hunt Question #4
When a magnet is in close range,
The inside of some metals will change.
The domains all turn to point the same way
And while the magnet is close that's how
they'll stay.

"As soon as I can get my writing hand free of this magnetic field I'll write it down!" I said. My left hand was at the very edge of the field and I pulled it away with all my strength and wrote: *When iron or steel is exposed to the magnetic field of a magnet, its domains line up.*

Mr. O'Neatly was pointing at us. "Now you can see what a magnetic field looks like. The iron filings create a swirl pattern that shows us the magnet's pull. There are more filings next to the ends of the magnet, and fewer in the middle. That's because the pull is strongest next to the ends, or poles of the magnet, and weaker in the middle. The field makes a circle around the bar magnet." I could see all of Mr. O'Neatly's kids writing down what he said. "Any questions?"

"No, sir," said the class in unison.

"Next we'll learn why magnets attract metal," said Mr. O'Neatly.

Great! We had already learned that, but as long as we were iron filings we'd be helping Mr. O'Neatly's students learn more about magnets. We had to escape!

CHAPTER 5

"OK, class," said Mr. O'Neatly, "now we're going to watch a videotape that will explain about magnetic domains."

"I wish we could have just learned about domains from a videotape," I whispered to Arnold.

"So does my stomach!" Arnold whispered back. His face was still green. I was glad that I knew about ordered domains, but I was tired of being an iron filing.

At that moment I saw Liz, who was still her normal size. She was crawling cautiously to the front of the classroom. She was carrying a big horseshoe magnet.

"If Liz can just crawl to the front of the class," said the Friz, "maybe she can attract us with her magnet, and then she can run off with us. Her magnet is bigger than the one under this paper and should be much stronger," the Friz explained. "Let's watch for an opportunity."

At that moment, the lights went out and Andrew moved the cardboard away from his bar magnet. Then he set us down on a desk, far from the magnet. We were free of its force!

"Now, class, join hands and make a chain since it's dark. I want to be ready when Liz comes. We need to make sure we all go together," said Ms. Frizzle.

I reached out and tried to grab Arnold's hand, and he reached over for mine. But all of a sudden, our iron-filing bodies moved apart with an irresistible force. "What . . . !" I yelled. It must be more magnetism, but where was it coming from? We were far from Andrew's magnet.

I looked around at the rest of the class. Everyone was flying away from his or her partner except for D.A. and Phoebe. D.A. was

reaching toward Phoebe's feet, and they flew together!

"Watch D.A. and Phoebe," said the Friz. "That's the way to do it!"

"You have to line up with your opposite ends facing," D.A. called out over her head. At that moment, Tim grabbed D.A.'s feet.

Arnold and I both rotated ourselves. Then our iron-filing feet came too close together. We flew apart again! Now half the class was stuck together and half were still apart. Ralphie had a hold of Keesha's feet next to us.

"You have to grab his feet with your arms, so the opposite poles come together," said Ralphie.

"That's right, class. Remember that you have two poles. Your hands are the north pole and your feet are the south pole," said Ms. Frizzle.

I stayed where I was. Arnold

scooted down so his head was close to my feet. Before he was completely in line we flew together with that same magical force. Magnetism! Everyone was now lining up into one long chain, head to feet. I reached for Ralphie's sneakers and *whoosh*! We were stuck together.

"Good job, class. You've discovered that magnets must attach by opposite poles," said the Friz. "Because we are magnetized, we now have north and south poles."

Opposites Attract

by Tim

Every magnet has a north pole and a south pole. If you put two magnets together with both their north poles facing each other, they will repel each other. And if both their south poles are facing, they will repel each other. Only opposite poles will attract each other, north to south.

"Hey!" I said, looking at my scavenger hunt list. "I think we know the answer to number five."

Scavenger Hunt Question #5
We're in each magnet.
Here is your big clue:
One is north, one is south,
Together we are two.
What are we?

"Magnets have north and south poles," said Tim.

"They certainly do," said Ms. Frizzle.

"And that's our answer!" I said. *Magnets have two poles, north on one end and south on the other.* I made a note of the answer in my mind since I couldn't write it down yet. I couldn't pull my hands from Ralphie's feet!

When I looked up I could see Liz approaching through the darkened classroom. Now all she had to do was grab us with her horseshoe magnet and take us away. Then we could get busy winning the scavenger hunt!

We were ahead! We were done with the question on poles and Mr. O'Neatly's class hadn't even read that one yet.

But at that moment Mr. O'Neatly turned the lights back on. We froze in our places. Liz scooted under Andrew's chair. "Class, the video will have to wait. We have a visitor."

To my horror, Mr. O'Neatly was looking at us again. Then he came over to the desk and started brushing our chain of iron filings into his hand. We'd been so close to escaping!

Then, to my surprise, he threw us on the floor. How disorderly! I thought he didn't like things on the floor.

"I have invited Mr. Broom, our head of maintenance, to do a demonstration." Mr. O'Neatly sounded pleased that Mr. Broom was on time. He liked things to happen right on schedule.

Footsteps were coming toward us. They stopped in front of us. I looked up the giant legs, and there was Mr. Broom. And in his hand was a vacuum cleaner!

"Mr. Broom will demonstrate a common

household appliance, and we will look at diagrams that show how magnets are a part of this appliance. Ms. Frizzle's class has also been given the same set of diagrams, but I asked Mr. Broom to be sure to come here first," Mr. O'Neatly boomed above us. He winked at his class and Andrew smirked.

"This does not look good!" said Arnold. I had to agree with him.

"So, Mr. O'Neatly asked Mr. Broom to come here first! This is supposed to be a friendly contest," said the Friz. She had a funny look in her eyes. "Class, it's time to get serious."

Mr. Broom leaned over and pushed the switch on the vacuum cleaner. "There's nothing like a clean sweep!" shouted the Friz.

That was the last thing I heard before the roar of the vacuum cleaner blotted out all sound. Our entire class of iron filings was sucked into the black mouth of the sweeper.

CHAPTER 6

"Everybody here?" Ms. Frizzle's voice called out in the darkness. She did a roll call, and everybody answered.

"Achoo!"

"Achoo!"

"Achoo!"

We were in the dirt bag of the sweeper and it was dusty in there! I felt for Arnold, but we were no longer attached. The force of the sweeper must have jumbled up our domains and we weren't magnetic anymore.

"We'll never win now," shouted Arnold above the roar of the vacuum.

Why a Temporary Magnet
is Temporary

by Ralphie

When a piece of iron is exposed to a magnet, its domains line up in the same direction. If a paper clip is turned into a temporary magnet, its domains have been lined up. If you bump a paper clip or needle against the table, it rejumbles the domains. Then the paper clip is no longer a magnet. Heating up a temporary magnet will also jumble its domains so it loses its magnetic pull.

"You never know," came the Friz's voice from somewhere in the dark.

"Ms. Frizzle's right. We may make a sweeping discovery," I said.

"Carlos!" groaned the class, as usual.

"We need the remote," said Ms. Frizzle. "Has anyone seen my bag?"

We hadn't seen anything since we'd been in the vacuum cleaner. It was too dark. But I felt something lumpy under me. At first I thought it was Arnold, but it was the bag.

"I found it!" I yelled.

"Good work, Carlos," said the Friz. "Can you reach in and turn on the remote?"

My hand located the remote and I flicked the switch. The whole place filled with light.

"Thank goodness!" I said, feeling relieved as I saw everyone's dusty faces.

Ms. Frizzle cleared her throat. I had the feeling she was getting ready to ask a teacherly question. And I was right.

"Who knows what Mr. O'Neatly meant about the sweeper being run with magnets?" she asked.

No one knew the answer.

"Well, then, we'll just have to take a look," said our teacher. "Follow me, class."

We ran after Ms. Frizzle. Wherever she was going had to be better than this dusty place.

The sound of the motor got louder and

louder. Ms. Frizzle slipped into a crevice and we were right behind her. We were inside the sweeper's motor! Something in the middle was spinning around so fast we couldn't see anything but a blur. We flattened ourselves against the walls. We didn't want to get caught up in that whirling thing.

I looked down at the remote and saw a button marked SLOW. Without thinking I punched it. Gradually the whirling crawled to a slow pace. The roaring sound got a lot quieter, and we could see the motor's parts. We even thought we saw magnets.

All wrapped up
by Keesha

If you wrap a coil of wire around an iron bar and then send energy through the wire, the iron bar becomes a powerful magnet—called an electromagnet.

Sure enough, there were two electro-magnets in the motor. One was attached to a part that did not move. The other was attached to a part in the middle that was spinning slowly around.

From *All about Magnets*
Moving and Non–moving Parts

A simple motor basically has two parts. One does not move: This is called the stator. The other spins, or rotates: This is the rotor.

"Remember how the poles of magnets attract and repel each other?" asked Ms. Frizzle.

"Yes, north poles push other north poles away from themselves. But they pull south poles toward themselves," said Wanda.

"Magnets can make each other move," said Phoebe.

"Is that how magnetism makes the rotor turn?" asked Tim.

"That must be how it works, Tim," said D.A., reading the book. "It says here that the north pole of the stator magnet pushes away the north pole of the rotor magnet."

"And then it pulls the rotor's south pole toward itself. That starts the rotor going around," said Ralphie.

"But wouldn't the rotor just stop once the opposite poles were facing each other?" asked Keesha.

"That's what alternating current is for," said the Friz. "It keeps the rotor turning."

"So that's the answer to number six!" shouted Wanda.

Scavenger Hunt Question #6
These magnets work with electric power.
You can turn them off and on.
They make a motor run for hours,
But with no electricity, their power is gone.

From *All about Magnets*
Changing Direction

The electric current in the wires in our houses is called "alternating current," or "AC" for short. This means that it changes directions many times each second.

Every time the current changes, it changes the poles in the electromagnets. The north pole becomes south and the south pole becomes north. The changes keep the rotor moving. Just when the rotor has stopped with its south pole stuck to the sta-tor's north pole, the poles change. Now the stator's north is south, so it pushes the rotor's south pole away again. The changes to the stator's poles keep the rotor going around and around.

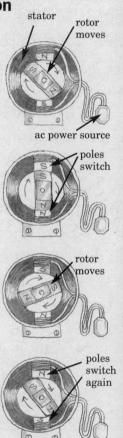

stator

rotor moves

ac power source

poles switch

rotor moves

poles switch again

"It's obvious!" I said, and I wrote: *The kind of magnet that uses electric current and creates motors is an electromagnet.*

For a while, we watched the rotor turning. It looked pretty cool spinning like that. Then I wondered about something.

"But how does the spinning rotor make a sweeper pick up dirt?" I asked Ms. Frizzle.

"Let's go see!" she said, and she took off again. We jumped up and followed.

The rotor was attached to a metal bar called a shaft. The shaft ran outside the motor and was attached to a fan.

"See? The turning of the rotor makes the blades of the fan turn," said Ms. Frizzle.

"I get it," said Arnold. "The fan pulls air into the vacuum bag." We could feel a gentle breeze blowing into the sweeper.

"And when the air comes in, dirt and dust come in with it," said Wanda.

Motes of dust danced in the breeze.

Ms. Frizzle reached over and took the remote. She pushed a button that said FAST. Uh-oh. We heard the roar of the motor again, and the gentle breeze became a hurricane! We were swept into the dirt bag again.

"Achoo!"

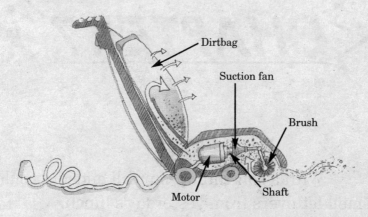

Then, just as suddenly, we heard a click. The roar stopped and the wind died. Mr. Broom must have turned off the vacuum cleaner.

"Whoa!" yelled everyone as we were suddenly lifted up. We slid backward and poured out of an opening. Mr. Broom was emptying the dirt bag.

"Help!" yelled Tim.

A strong force was pulling us. I tried to stop, but I couldn't. The force wasn't magnetism, and it wasn't suction. It was plain old gravity. We were falling.

CHAPTER 7

With a soft thump, our fall ended. I could smell leftovers from yesterday's lunch.

"Stay calm, class," the Friz called. "We've hit bottom."

"Yes, the bottom of the trash can!" I called out.

"Carlos, is that you? Do you still have the remote?" asked Ms. Frizzle.

"Got it!" I called back.

"Now press the button with the picture of a little person on it."

I looked at the remote. There were all sorts of interesting buttons with interesting pictures, but I figured now was not the time to experiment. I found the button with the picture of the person and pressed it.

I looked down and my arms and legs were attached to my normal body again. I looked around and could see Keesha and Wanda standing up and brushing themselves off. Then I saw the Friz and the rest of the class. They were back to their own shapes, but were still miniature. We ran toward one another and Ms. Frizzle took her satchel off her shoulder.

"No more iron man for me!" I said.

"First order of business is to get out of this trash chute before Mr. Broom empties it into a Dumpster. Quick, put these on!"

The Friz was taking some half-boots out of her bag — they were toes only, with a bar magnet attached to the front.

The individual boots buckled right over the front of our shoes. They weren't that heavy. Then the Friz took out some gloves, with the same metal bar attached to the front. We all began putting the boots and gloves on. "These are grippers," said the Friz. "The bottoms are equipped with strong magnets."

I had my boots on. I tried to lift my foot and nearly fell over. It was sticking to the metal bottom of the chute.

"You need to peel your foot off slowly sideways," the Friz explained.

That's when I noticed that the sides of the grippers were curved. I could roll the gripper off the metal to break its hold.

"How are these boots and gloves going to help us?" asked Tim.

Gripping Technology
by Arnold

Grippers allow workers to scale offshore oil rigs, bridges, towers, and steel girders in construction sites. Each gripper weighs only 1.5 pounds, but provides 500 pounds of attractive force or more to a steel surface. The curved sides help you rock the gripper away from the wall to move it.

"Just watch and learn!" the Friz called out. With a clang she reached the edge of the floor, put one foot up on the metal wall, and began walking straight up the steep slope.

We were just getting used to walking in the grippers when we heard an awful grating sound. The top of the trash chute opened up, and more garbage began tumbling down the chute.

"He's emptying the garbage!" screamed Phoebe. "Run before we get buried!" We all began shakily moving across the floor. We all were waving our arms in crazy circles to keep our balance. One by one, we made it to the wall of the chute and started walking straight up. It was hard work.

It was such hard work that about halfway up we reached a little ledge and the Friz called a halt.

I leaned against the wall and took out the scavenger hunt list. "Hey," I said. "I think I see another answer!"

Scavenger Hunt Question #7

Magnets can run motors,
But you know that is not all.
With these special boots and gloves
They help workers climb the wall.

I wrote down: *Workers climb steel walls wearing industrial grippers.*

Only three more questions to go. I was so excited, I felt my energy come back. "Let's keep going, guys," I said. "We don't want to throw this opportunity away — with the garbage!"

We began climbing up the rest of the trash chute. Phoebe was the last person out. We sat on the floor, took off our boots, and handed them to the Friz.

She somehow crammed them all in her bag. My legs and arms felt like I'd been playing kickball all day! We were all lying on the ground rubbing our legs and arms, too.

"We don't want to sit here collecting dust," said the Friz. "Up, class, we've got to win the race!" We painfully got to our feet.

CHAPTER 8

We looked to the right; we looked to the left. We were so small, we could only see endless walls.

"Does anyone remember where the trash chute is in relation to our classroom?" asked the Friz. We all looked blank.

"You're saying we're lost, Ms. Frizzle?" said Ralphie.

"Well, let's just say it would help if we knew if our classroom was on the north side of the school building or the south side," Ms. Frizzle replied.

We were all silent.

"Then we may be lost," said the Friz.

We started to panic, when I thought of something.

"Hey! Remember the signs on the walls of our room — the ones left over from our geography unit? They said north, south, east, and west."

"That's right, Carlos," said Dorothy Ann. "The one over Ms. Frizzle's desk was west."

"And the windows were north," said Tim.

"Since our room is at the end of the hall, our room must be in the northwest part of the school," said Arnold. He looked really excited.

"Good calculating, class," said the Friz.

"But how does that help us?" I asked.

Arnold's smile disappeared. He started thinking. "If we had a compass we could find out which way is northwest and go there," he said, smiling again.

"But we don't have a compass," I pointed out.

Arnold's smile went away again.

"I know," said D.A. "We can build our own compass!"

Ms. Frizzle had a cup and cork, but no magnetized needle. We needed all three to make a compass.

Something was pricking in the back of my mind. . . . Suddenly I remembered. "I've got one!" I shouted. "I pinned my shirt closed with my magnetized needle." I carefully pulled it out of the buttonhole. I knew if I shook it, the domains might resettle and the magnetism would be gone.

"Good work, Carlos," said Ms. Frizzle. "I always said you were a sharp one!"

"I'll fill the cup with water," said Keesha. She ran to the drinking fountain. There was luckily a leak coming out the bottom. Keesha filled the cup and ran back.

Ms. Frizzle handed Keesha the cork and the needle. Keesha floated the flat disk of cork on top of the water. Then she carefully set my needle on the cork. It spun around a little and then finally pointed down the hall.

"Aha," said the Friz. "The needle will always point north-south because it follows the line of Earth's magnetic field."

"Wow," said Ralphie. "Magnets really are everywhere! Even Earth is a magnet."

"That's exactly right," said the Friz. "Now, we know our class is on the north side of the building, and I know that the trash chute is on the south side. The base of the needle is pointing at the trash chute, so the tip must be pointing north. Follow that needle!"

"And now we have the answer to number eight," said Phoebe.

The Magnetic Planet Earth
by Carlos

It's no coincidence that Earth has two poles, just like a magnet. The molten iron in the center of Earth gives the planet its own magnetic field. A compass needle will line up with Earth's field and point to the north.

The magnetic poles are not exactly the same as the geographic poles you see on a globe, but they are close.

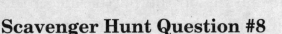

Scavenger Hunt Question #8

When you are lost you look at me.
On my face there is an S, W, N, and E.
Only with magnetism will I point the
   right way.
If you trust me, I won't lead you astray.

"It's what we just built," said Tim.

"A compass, of course," I said. I wrote: *A compass uses a magnet to show which way is north.*

Animal Magnetism
by Phoebe

People have always wondered how birds and sea animals know which way to migrate in the winter. Sometimes animals travel thousands of miles, and they always know exactly where to go. Scientists think they may feel Earth's magnetic field. Tiny pieces of magnetite have been found in certain creatures, such as bees and butterflies. These animals may be living compasses!

CHAPTER 9

"Hey, before we take off for the other side of the building, we should read the next riddle," I said to the rest of the class.

Scavenger Hunt Question #9
Deep inside a VCR and TV,
There are many magnets to be found.
How do magnets play a part
In recording tapes of sight and sound?

"Tapes of sight and sound?" Wanda asked. "Like movies?"

"You're probably right, Wanda," Tim said. "Let's think about it while we're on the move."

We took off, thinking about how magnets might record tapes. It was a really tough question.

As we ran down the hall, we came to an intersection. The needle showed us we needed to keep going straight. As we ran down the hall we could see the door to Mr. O'Neatly's class ahead.

By the time we got there, we were panting. We stood in the doorway and looked inside. At the front of the classroom, a videotape was playing.

"Hey, our scavenger riddle," D.A. exclaimed.

"Put on these magnet-detecting glasses and tell me what you see," said the Friz. She was handing out sets of dark glasses.

I put mine on and looked inside Mr. O'Neatly's classroom. On all the desks were bright green shapes. "The bright green things must be magnets," I exclaimed.

"I'll give you a green light for that," said the Friz.

"Look at the video!" said Wanda.

The entire TV set was covered in bright green. The television set and VCR had bunches of green blobs in them, too.

Stacked on top of the VCR were several videotapes, and they were green as well.

"Wow!" said Ralphie. "Are those all magnets?"

"Yes. Magnets are used to power the speakers and the motor and they also create the pictures on the screen," explained the Friz.

"So are TV sets magnetic?" asked D.A.

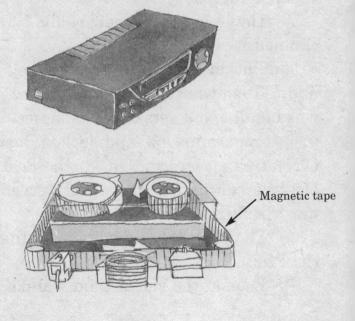

Magnetic tape

"Televisions contain about two pounds of magnets, which makes them rather attractive," joked the Friz.

"But what about the tapes? What is the answer to the riddle?" I asked.

Ms. Frizzle continued, "All the sound and the pictures are stored in billions of tiny magnets that are stuck in the tape."

"That's great!" I said. I wrote: *Videotape is magnetic. The picture and sound are stored on magnets on the tape.*

The video in Mr. O'Neatly's room was explaining compasses.

"Great!" Wanda whispered. "They must still be behind us! We're almost done!"

"OK, then," said the Friz, "we need to answer the last question and get back to the science lab, or Mr. O'Neatly's class will win."

"What a *repelling* idea," I said. The thought of Mr. O'Neatly's class winning again made us all nervous.

At that moment we heard something dreadful. "OK, class," said Mr. O'Neatly. "We've answered all the questions we can.

Let's proceed in an orderly fashion to the science lab."

We flattened ourselves back against the hallway walls as we heard the sound of chairs being pushed back and giant footsteps approaching the door. We were still so small. How would we ever catch up?

CHAPTER 10

As soon as Mr. O'Neatly's class had filed out the door, the Friz said, "Carlos, do you have the list?"

I waved it in the air. The Friz pointed toward the science lab and said, "Then let's go! The last answer is at the science lab."

We started down the hall, and as we ran we felt ourselves getting bigger. As soon as we reached our full size, we rounded the corner and caught up with Mr. O'Neatly's class.

"Wait a minute," Mr. O'Neatly called out loudly. "Remember, no running in the halls!" He didn't look happy to see us.

I stopped running and started walking as fast as I could. Someone was keeping pace with me. It was Andrew! His mouth was shut tight and his eyebrows were pulled down over his eyes.

We rounded the other corner. Andrew and I were in front of the crowd, still neck and neck. Nobody was saying a word, and I could hear Andrew start to breathe hard. Then I saw the science lab. *Faster, faster,* I thought. We were so close to finally beating Mr. O'Neatly's class!

Andrew and I came to a stop in front of the science lab door. It was closed but my hand was first on the knob. I turned it — it was locked!

I rattled the knob, but it did no good. "Here, let me," said Andrew, pushing my hand aside. He tried to open the door, but it still wouldn't budge. "It's locked," he said, looking at me with surprise. I shrugged.

"I guess we can't get in," said Mr. O'Neatly with a chuckle. He and the Friz

looked at each other and I saw him wink. They knew it would be locked! They were up to something.

"There must be a way!" I said to Andrew. I began feeling around the edges of the door. He got down on his knees and looked under the door.

"There's something there!" he said.

I got down next to him. "It's a key," I said.

"But how do we get it?" he asked. We looked at each other. That's when I remembered there was still one riddle left. We looked at the last question on our scavenger hunt list.

Final Scavenger Hunt Task

You are almost done,
But you have come to a closed door.
If you can use your magnet logic,
You'll find pizza and soda and more!

"We need a magnet!" we said at the same time.

"Anyone have a magnet?" I asked the crowd of kids behind us. Someone passed a bar magnet forward. I gently slid the magnet under the door and felt a ping as the key stuck to it. I pulled out the magnet and held it up to Andrew. He removed the key from the magnet. It fit right into the lock and together we pushed the door open and stepped into the lab. The tables were covered with hot pizzas!

"I guess it's a tie," said Andrew with a smile.

I smiled back.

"We'll just have to have a joint pizza party," said Mr. O'Neatly. Andrew and I shook hands and behind us both classes cheered. We'd finally won something (well, tied), and it would be even more fun to eat pizza with Mr. O'Neatly's class.

"Hey, what's that on the refrigerator?" Ms. Frizzle asked Mr. O'Neatly.

"Oh, just some bus toy I found on the floor," said Mr. O'Neatly. He looked embarrassed. "I was going to put it in the lost-and-found," he said, heading toward the miniature Magic School Bus.

"Actually, that's mine," said Ms. Frizzle. She plucked the tiny bus off the refrigerator door and gave Mr. O'Neatly a big smile. "Thank you so much for finding it for me! I know I can always trust you to tidy up."

Mr. O'Neatly looked very proud.

Carlos's Scavenger Hunt List
Scavenger Hunt Question #1
A magnet picks me up.
A magnet holds me high.
I'm not paper, wood, or rubber.
I'm not plastic — what am I?
Answer: Metals that contain iron and steel stick to magnets.

Scavenger Hunt Question #2
We look the same as rocks,
But we don't act the same.
We are natural magnets.
Can you guess our name?
Answer: Magnetite is a rock that is a natural magnet.

Scavenger Hunt Question #3
Not all magnets start on the ground.
Not all magnets have to be found.
When you do this very easy chore,
You can use one magnet to make many more.
Answer: If you stroke a needle with a magnet

in one direction, the needle will become a magnet.

Scavenger Hunt Question #4
When a magnet is in close range,
The inside of some metals will change.
The domains all turn to point the same way
And while the magnet is close that's how
    they'll stay.
Answer: Magnetic domains have their molecules lined up to create magnetic fields.

Scavenger Hunt Question #5
We're in each magnet.
Here is your big clue:
One is north, one is south,
Together we are two.
What are we?
Answer: Magnets have two poles, north on one end and south on the other.

Scavenger Hunt Question #6
These magnets work with electric power.
You can turn them off and on.

They make a motor run for hours,
But with no electricity, their power is gone.
Answer: The kind of magnet that uses electric current and creates motors is an electromagnet.

Scavenger Hunt Question #7
Magnets can run motors,
But you know that is not all.
With these special boots and gloves
They help workers climb the wall.
Answer: Workers climb steel walls wearing industrial grippers.

Scavenger Hunt Question #8
When you are lost you look at me.
On my face there is an S, W, N, and E.
Only with magnetism will I point the right way.
If you trust me, I won't lead you astray.
Answer: A compass uses a magnet to show which way is north.

Scavenger Hunt Question #9
Deep inside a VCR and TV,
There are many magnets to be found.
How do magnets play a part
In recording tapes of sight and sound?
*Answer: Videotape is magnetic. The picture
and sound are stored on magnets on the tape.*

Magic Show

While we ate pizza together, Andrew and I came up with a great idea. Our classes could put on a magic act together for the school talent show! We could think of a bunch of magnetic magic tricks.

Ms. Frizzle said we should all work with a partner from the other class. I looked at Andrew and he looked at me . . . and a great partnership was born.

On the day of the show, Andrew and I came to school with black top hats, and together we announced all the acts in the show. Andrew's hat had the word MAGNETISM written on it in big letters. Mine said ATTRACTION, and guess what. I spelled it right!

Here are all the magic tricks Andrew and I performed during class.

MAGNET-MAGIC TRICKS

King of the Compass

Sew or tape a magnet into your sleeve. Then explain to the audience that with your powers of thought, you will move a compass needle. Show them a large compass, and whenever you tell them you are moving the needle, pass your arm with the hidden magnet over it!

Sticky Metal

Tape a magnet to your knee, sit down at a table, and cross your legs so that the magnet is against the bottom of the tabletop. Lay a paper clip on the table just above the magnet. Then place a fork on the paper clip. Now, gently lift the fork and paper clip from the table. They will stick together. Shake the fork and the paper clip will fall off. Ask someone else to try sticking them together — without a magnet, they can't!